MIIB
MEN IN BLACK II

THE JOKE BOOK

1 2 3 4 5 6 7 8 9 10
❖
First Edition

www.harperchildrens.com
www.MenInBlack.com

MIIB
MEN IN BLACK II
THE JOKE BOOK

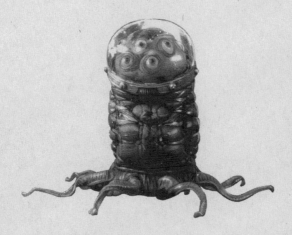

By Z. L. Katz

Photography by Melinda Sue Gordon

HarperFestival®
A Division of HarperCollins*Publishers*

BASIC BLACK

What do you get when you cross agents with a duck?

Men in Quack.

✤ What do you get when you cross agents with burlap?
Men in Sack.

✤ What do you call a pile of agents?
Men in Stack.

✤ What do you call the teachers at the bureau?
Mentors in Black.

✤ What do you call agents who have experienced the neuralyzer?
Men in Blackout.

🪐 What do you call the Men in Black after they save the planet?
Men intact. *Whew!*

🪐 What do you call agents when you bring them to school?
Men in Backpack.

🪐 What do you call agents who are lost in space?
Men in Black Holes.

🪐 What do you call agents trained in karate?
Men in Black Belt.

How did the Men in Black punish Jeff for violating his zone restrictions?
He was *under*grounded.

What do you call agents who get hurt while on duty?
Men in Black and Blue.

Who are the Men in Black and Yellow?
Agents posing as New York City taxi drivers.

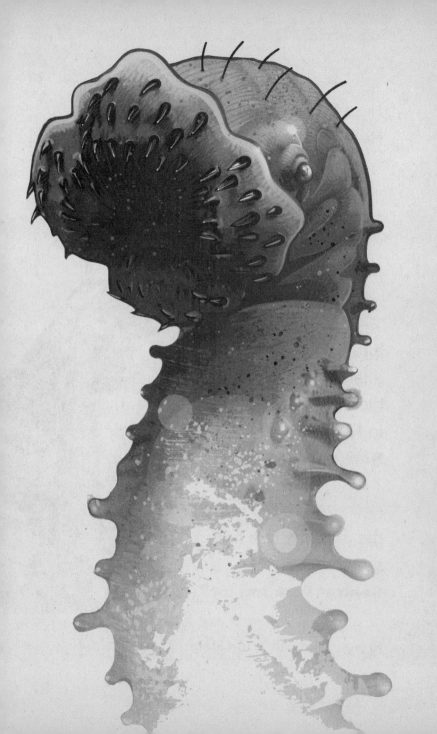

🌀 How did Jay feel about living in New York City?

He felt a real sense of alien nation.

🌀 What did the alien say to the garbage collector?

"Take me to your litter."

🌀 Where did one alien choose to hide his spaceship in New York City?

Rocket-feller Center.

🌀 Where did most of the aliens leave their spaceships?

Central Park-ing lot.

AGEN-C HUMOR

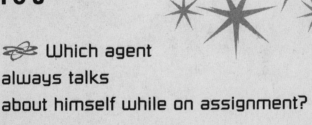

✺ Which 3 agents are always in debt?
I O U

✺ Which agent always talks about himself while on assignment?
I

✺ Which 2 agents are always fine with their assignments?
O K

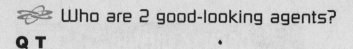 Who are 2 good-looking agents?
Q T

 Which agent is always full of wonder about alien life-forms?
G

Which 2 agents are constantly out of ammunition?

M T

Which 3 agents went off together on an assignment and can't be found?

M I A

Which 3 agents are the worst at undercover surveillance?

I C U

Which 3 agents used to work in Russia?

K G B

Which 4 agents are happiest when the weekend comes?

T G I F

✺ Which 3 agents record every detail of their cases?

V C R

✺ Which agent outlines everything at a crime scene?

X (He marks the spot!)

✺ Which agent always asks questions during an investigation?

Y

DON'T KNOCK IT TILL YOU'VE TRIED IT

Knock, knock.
Who's there?
Trash can.
Trash can who?
"Trash can taste good," says Jeff.

Knock, knock.
Who's there?
Planet.
Planet who?
Planet better next time so we don't have to rush to save the Earth!

Knock, knock.
Who's there?
Al.
Al who?
Al-ien.

Knock, knock.

Who's there?

Wormwood.

Wormwood who?

Wormwood help save Earth if you just ask!

Jay: Knock, knock.

Laura: Who's there?

Jay: Pizza.

Laura: Pizza who?

Jay: Pizza meet you.

Charlie: Knock, knock.

Scrad: Who's there?

Charlie: Head.

Scrad: Head who?

Charlie: Head for cover—Serleena's looking for us!

Knock, knock.
Who's there?
Beak.
Beak who?
Beak careful. There's a bird alien behind you.

CANINE PROFILING

✻ Why is it easy for the other agents to find Frank? **Because he's always tailed.**

✻ How did Frank look to the other agents? **Pug-ly.**

🌀 What did Jay say to Zed when Zed gave him a canine partner?
"Don't pug me."

🌀 What do you call it when Frank chases and catches other dogs?
Dog tag.

🌀 What do you tell Frank to do when he's on a stakeout?
Watch, dog.

🌀 What is it called when Frank is chasing aliens?
Dogged pursuit.

What is it called when Frank catches a rogue alien?

Dog collar.

What happens when Frank gets overheated chasing aliens?

He becomes a hot dog.

How do you sneak Frank out of a restaurant?

In a doggie bag.

FOR NO EARTHLY REASON

What's an out-of-this-world hobby?

A space craft.

⚛ What goes around and around and never seems to get anywhere?
A planet.

⚛ How did Kay feel about post-office work?
It had his stamp of approval.

⚛ Why was Kay working in the post office?
He was a first-class male.

⚛ How did Kay find his experience with the deneuralyzer?
Memorable.

⚛ What is Kay's favorite breakfast food?
Special K cereal.

✺ What is it called when Jay dashes across a busy Manhattan street?
Jaywalking.

✺ What is Jay's favorite animal?
Jaybird.

✺ What kind of pet would Kay like to have?
K-9.

✺ How did Kay feel about using the Noisy Cricket?
He had a blast.

✺ What does a little Noisy Cricket look like?
A son of a gun.

☀ If the De-Atomizer is a Series Four weapon, then what is the Noisy Cricket?

A miniseries.

☀ What do you call it when Jeff squeezes into a subway car?

Outta space.

☀ What kind of pizzas did Ben make?

Ones with extra saucer.

☀ Why did Serleena go to the pizza place?

She wanted to treat herself to something Light.

☀ How would you measure the robot alien creature?

In inches. He doesn't have any feet.

What did the robot alien say when he spotted Jay?

Eyes see you.

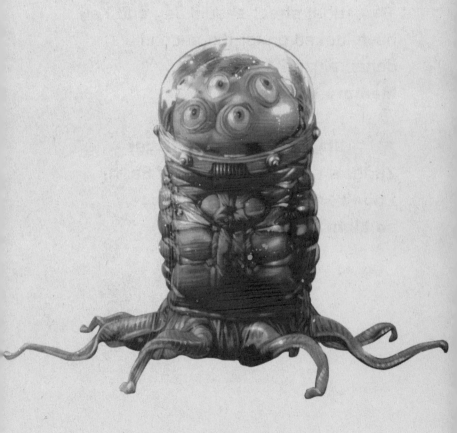

✺ Why do Zed and Frank seem so formal?

It could be the black tie and tail.

✺ What street should Jay and Kay have looked on for the second deneuralyzer?

Memory Lane.

✺ Why was it so hard to get Zartha's power source off of Earth?

I don't know. After all, it was so Light.

 Why should you never insult an alien?

You might hurt its feelers.

 How did the alien feel when it was told it had to go into outer space?
Star-tled!

 What do you call a starship that drips water?
A crying saucer.

How does an alien count to 23?
On its fingers.

Why did Jay take a vacation?
His boss Zed he needed one.

 Why shouldn't you ask this alien about her feathers?

It's a ticklish subject.

✺ What is this alien's...

...favorite game?
Eye-Spy.

...favorite
tv show?
*Gilligan's
Eye-land.*

...favorite food?
Eye-scream.

...favorite
vacation spot?
**The Eye-full
Tower.**

...favorite flower?
Eye-ris.

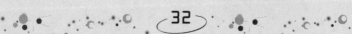

 Why does this alien not need glasses?
He has 20-20-20 vision.

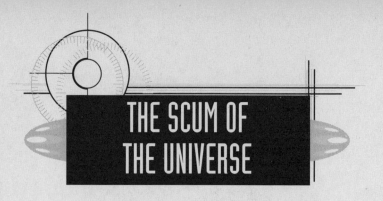

THE SCUM OF
THE UNIVERSE

✦ **What did Serleena consider herself to be?**
A model alien.

⦰ **What was she really?**
The root of all evil.

⦰ **Why should Charlie have been smarter?**
Because he was *a head* of the pack.

⦰ **How did Charlie feel about Scrad?**
He was nothing to sneeze at.

⦰ **How accommodating was Jay to the aliens in Jeebs' pawn shop?**

He bent over backward for them.

⦰ **What does Serleena think human ears are?**
Root canals.

✺ What's sad but true about Scrad and Charlie?

Two heads aren't better than one.

✺ How does Charlie support Scrad?

He backs him up all the time.

✦ When do Scrad and Charlie go to a baseball game?
When it's a doubleheader.

✦ **Scrad: You know, you have a great head on your shoulders.**
Charlie: Really?
Scrad: Yeah, mine!

Knock, knock.
Who's there?
Colin.
Colin who?
Colin the Men in Black. Serleena is on the loose!

GALAXY DEFENDERS

⚛ What did Jay say to Kay when they popped out of the drain onto 42nd Street?
"You look flushed."

⚛ How did Jay feel after being flushed out onto 42nd Street?
Drained.

⚛ What did Agent Jay say when Agent Kay opened the locker in Grand Central Terminal?
"It's a small world after all."

✧ If the 8-foot-tall alien could have played basketball, what would his name have been?
Kareem Abdul–Jarra-bar.

✧ What was it called when Serleena's spacecraft rammed into Jay's car?

A galaxy-defender bender.

✧ What did Jay need to navigate his car through the subway?
Tunnel vision.

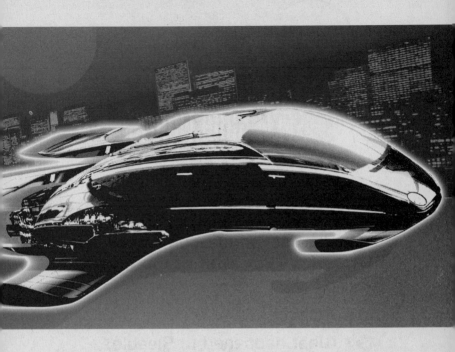

✺ What did Jeff say when he saw Serleena in her spacecraft?

"Pleased to eat you."

LOOKING FOR A FEW GOOD WORMS

〰 Are the Worm Guys brave? **Not really. They split at the first sign of danger.**

〰 What happened to Sleeble, Neeble, Mannix, and the others when they began to fit into New York City life? **They became Earth worms.**

〰 What did the Alpha Team Bravo worms say to the enemy crickets? **"Don't bug us."**

❀ Why did Alpha Team Bravo crawl around in the ceilings of Men in Black headquarters?

They needed to vent.

❀ What kind of fighters are Alpha Team Bravo?

They're gunny worms.

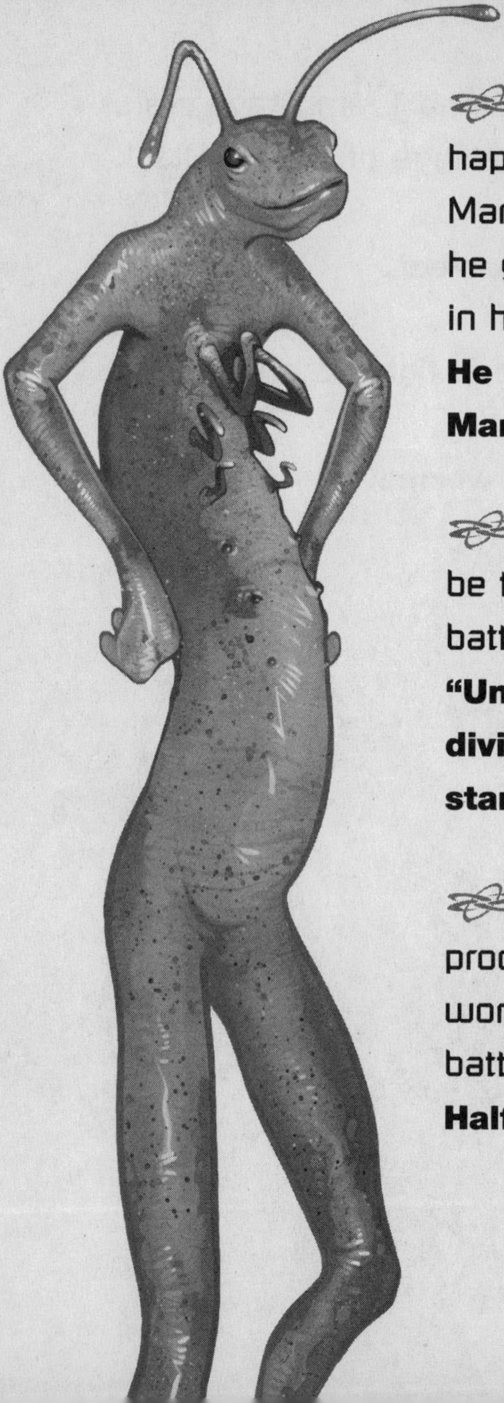

What happened to Mannix when he got chopped in half?

He opened a Mannix annex.

What should be the worms' battle cry?

"United we fall, divided we stand."

What dairy product makes worms stronger in battle?

Half-and-half.

 How did Sleeble handle navigating Jay's car while Serleena chased it?

He wormed his way out of it.

FLIGHT TO THE FINISH

What did Kay say when he took the Pulsar from the locker?
"Watch out!"

How did Laura look with the bracelet on her wrist?
Charm-ing.

What time is it when you finish reading the last joke?
Time to go "off book."

Knock, knock.
Who's there?
Men.
Men who?
**Men't to tell
you this is
almost the
last joke.**

What's the best way to finish this book?
Just watch the neuralyzer!

Xath all folks!